Minnie's Slumber Party

Written by Cindy West

A GOLDEN BOOK • NEW YORK
Western Publishing Company, Inc., Racine, Wisconsin 53404

 Library of Congress Catalog Card Number: 89-82150 ISBN: 0-307-00081-8

MCMXCII

Minnie Mouse was very excited! In just a few hours she was going to have her first slumber party.

Minnie called Daisy to remind her to bring a sleeping bag. "The party's going to be such fun!" said Minnie. "All our friends from school will be coming!"

"Did you get lots of treats to eat?" Daisy asked.

"I'm going to get them right now," Minnie told her. "Bye-bye. See you later!"

Minnie rushed to the store and picked out delicious cookies and lots of chips. But just as she was leaving—CRASH!—her cart bumped into another!

"Oh, gosh, Minnie! I'm sorry." It was Penny, who had just recently moved to Minnie's neighborhood.

"May I help you carry your groceries home?" asked Penny.

"All right," agreed Minnie. Penny handed Minnie her groceries when they reached Minnie's front door.

"Thanks a lot," said Minnie.

"Oh, it was nothing," said Penny. "See you around, I guess."

Penny then went across the street to her house.

As Minnie unpacked all the treats she thought, "Now my friends will have plenty to eat. But what else can we do to have fun?"

Just then Minnie happened to glance out the window, and she saw Penny dancing on her porch. "Dancing! That's what we'll do!" Minnie decided. She quickly called up all her friends and asked them to bring their favorite music.

"Now I'll decorate the table with pretty flowers," said Minnie.

She picked lots of pink roses from her garden, but she couldn't seem to make a nice arrangement.

As Minnie struggled with the flowers Penny passed by on her roller skates. "Would you like me to help you?" she asked. "Sometimes I'm good at arranging flowers."

"Sure, I'd love it!" said Minnie.

Penny carefully cut the stems and took off the extra leaves. "Ouch!" she cried. "Those thorns always get me!"

"The flowers look beautiful!" Minnie said with a grin. "You did a terrific job!"

After Penny skated away, Minnie thought, "Now, I'd like to think of something new to do at my party. Maybe Daisy has a new game or something."

As Minnie rode over to Daisy's house she noticed that Penny was sitting in her garden making a pretty bracelet. "That's what we can all do!" Minnie thought. "We can make beaded jewelry!"

Minnie quickly rode over to the crafts store to buy lots of different colored beads and string.

Soon it was time for Minnie's party. All of her friends seemed to come at the same time!

Daisy and Amy brought lots of records. Stacy said, "I just learned a new dance to teach everyone."

Colette and Cheryl brought a plate of brownies. "This is going to be a great party!" said Cheryl.

As Minnie was greeting all of her friends she noticed Penny jumping rope. "I love to jump rope!" Minnie said. "Why don't we join Penny and do that first?"

So they did! Penny wasn't a very good jumper. But she knew such a funny jump-rope rhyme, she made everyone laugh! Penny sang,

"Two little girls sitting on a fence,
trying to make a dollar out of ninety-nine cents.
Do they need an A, B, C, or D?
No, all they need is one penny!"

Then everyone began rushing back to the party. "Well, see you," Penny said a little wistfully.

"Oh, my gosh!" said Minnie, looking back at her. "I've been so busy thinking of my old friends, I didn't notice I was making a *new* one!"

Minnie dashed back and grabbed Penny's hand. "Will you come to my party, Penny? Say yes! Oh, please say yes!"

"Of course I will!" Penny grinned at her. "I was really hoping you'd ask!"

So Penny packed her pajamas and records and ran back home with Minnie.

"Uh-oh," Penny said. "I don't have a sleeping bag."
"Don't worry!" said Minnie. "I've got an extra one!"

Then Minnie and her friends put on their music and sang along and danced. And when they made jewelry, Penny handed Minnie a special present.

"Wow," said Minnie. "This bracelet is just like yours."

"It's a friendship bracelet," said Penny, "for my new friend!"

Soon they all put on their pajamas and snuggled into their sleeping bags. Just before she closed her eyes, Minnie said, "It's great to have my old friends with me—and my terrific new friend, too!"